STAMPEDE!

Winter Weasel felt a shiver of excitement run through his body. He had practiced this part many times, but never before had he raced in front of the herd.

He turned his back to the great beasts and began to walk steadily toward the cliff. He did not need to look back to know that the buffaloes were following him. The sound of their hoofbeats told him that the stampede had begun.

Winter Weasel broke into a trot, and the buffaloes began to trot, too. They were about a mile from the cliff, and he knew that the next few minutes would be the most important ones in his life....

BUFFALO KILL
was originally published by Thomas Nelson & Sons.

Critics' Corner:

"...a swift tale of adventure" —*Virginia Kirkus Service*

"An outstanding book for illustration and story....The account of the mystical, ceremonious preparations for the dangerous maneuver creates rising suspense. The author's haunting drawings convey the expanse of the ancient West, and the spirit of its Indian inhabitants." —*Denver Post*

"A highly imaginative story of Winter Weasel, son of Gray Wolf the medicine man, who won his right to manhood by leading the autumn hunt for buffalo. Tribal rites are described with much warmth and understanding of the Blackfoot tribe. ...Recommended, especially, for school libraries where good material on Indian tribes is always in demand."
—*Library Journal* (especially recommended)

"With careful detailing of each step in the *piskun*, the story moves to a climax with suspense and a feeling of concern for Winter Weasel's safety and success...a particularly thorough and handsomely produced treatment. Animated pen-and-ink drawings add much to its lively atmosphere."
—*Horn Book*

About the Author and Illustrator:

GARDELL DANO CHRISTENSEN'S interest in wildlife and Indians began during his boyhood in Idaho. He studied at the Art Students' League, and is a professional sculptor of animals. For fifteen years he worked at the American Museum of Natural History in New York, collecting and mounting the animals in the famous African and North American halls. At present, Mr. Christensen is engaged in designing and constructing exhibits for the twenty-three historic sites operated by the office of the State Historian in the New York State Education Department.

BUFFALO KILL

BUFFALO KILL

Written and Illustrated by
Gardell Dano Christensen

AN ARCHWAY PAPERBACK
WASHINGTON SQUARE PRESS, INC. • NEW YORK

BUFFALO KILL

An Archway Paperback edition
1st printing .... January, 1968

Published by
Washington Square Press, Inc., 630 Fifth Avenue, New York, N.Y.

WASHINGTON SQUARE PRESS editions are distributed in the U.S. by Simon & Schuster, Inc., 630 Fifth Avenue, New York, N.Y. 10020 and in Canada by Simon & Schuster of Canada, Ltd., Richmond Hill, Ontario, Canada.

Copyright, ©, 1959 by Gardell Dano Christensen. All rights reserved. This Archway Paperback edition is published by arrangement with Thomas Nelson & Sons.
Printed in the U.S.A.

HISTORICAL SOCIETY OF MONTANA

FOREWORD

MANY BOOKS HAVE BEEN WRITTEN about the Indians after the coming of the white man to North America, but little is known of their life before then. Gardell Dano Christensen has chosen this unrecorded period as the setting for his book, *Buffalo Kill*.

The Blackfeet Indians roamed the Montana plains in those days. They were hunters and the buffalo was their principal source of food, clothing, and shelter. Before the white man came, these Indians had no horses and they had to lure a herd of buffaloes over a cliff in order to kill the animals in large numbers.

In 1952, I asked Mr. Christensen to come to Helena to make a diorama of the buffalo kill, or piskun, for one of the halls of the Historical Museum. We visited actual sites of piskuns and saw the circles in which the Indians danced and the piles of rocks which marked the "funnel" through which the animals were chased to the edge of the cliff.

I am glad that Mr. Christensen has put the story of a piskun into a book. His description of this important event in the lives of the Indians and his many pen-and-ink drawings will help young readers to a better understanding of a neglected segment of our western history.

K. Ross Toole, Director
Historical Society of Montana
Helena, Montana
August, 1958

To the Fires of the Wilderness around which I have learned so much, around which so much is still to be learned. May they burn forever.

CONTENTS

1. *The Coming of the Tribe*   3

2. *The Place of the Piskun*   21

3. *Moon Magic*   41

4. *Swift as Lightning and Loud as Thunder*   55

5. *The Stampede*   71

6. *The Prayer of Thanks*   93

7. *Enough for All*   101

BUFFALO KILL

CHAPTER ONE

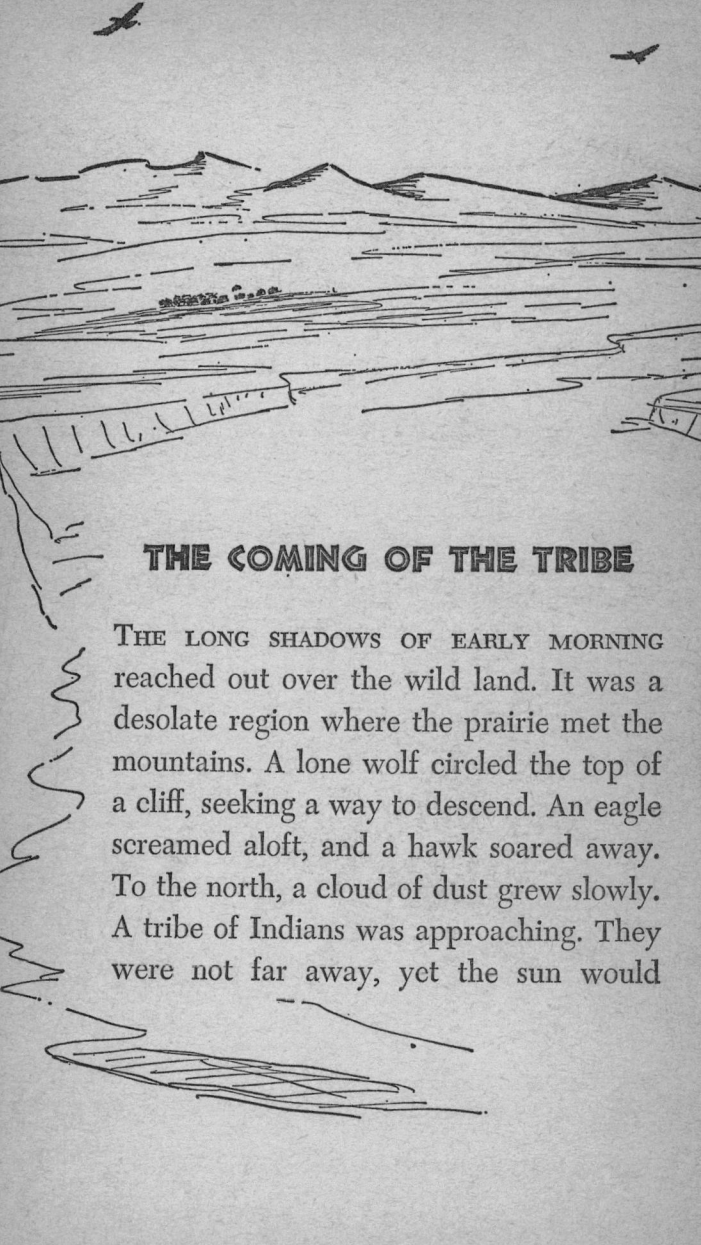

THE COMING OF THE TRIBE

THE LONG SHADOWS OF EARLY MORNING reached out over the wild land. It was a desolate region where the prairie met the mountains. A lone wolf circled the top of a cliff, seeking a way to descend. An eagle screamed aloft, and a hawk soared away. To the north, a cloud of dust grew slowly. A tribe of Indians was approaching. They were not far away, yet the sun would make half of its journey across the sky before they arrived at the place of the buffalo kill, for they must walk at the pace of a child. The whole tribe was coming.

Gray Wolf, the medicine chief, was leading. He knew that the little valley in the deep gorge between steep cliffs was waiting for his people, as it had waited each fall and spring for a thousand years. He had told the people how the waters talked to the rocks of the excitement that was to come; how the wind whispered to the willows that the summer was gone. He had told them that Mother Earth was ready to give food to her children for the long winter.

Gray Wolf was tall; his head was small, his shoulders wide. His bones were big, and the skin was tight and weather-worn over his lean muscles. He was naked except for a breechcloth and traveling moccasins. On his head was the buffalo cap with three red-tail hawk feathers on it. Around his neck hung the amulet of the buffalo.

Beside him walked his oldest son, Winter Weasel, a boy of twelve snows. Like his father, Winter Weasel wore only a loincloth of calfskin. His moccasins were made of the well-tanned heels of a young buffalo's hind legs. They were made for traveling, with an extra sole of rawhide; a simple design worked in porcupine quills covered the tops. His head was shaved except for the lone scalp lock. From it hung, on both sides of his face, two ermine skins, the symbol of his name. Two sparrow-hawk feathers hung loosely from the

black scalp lock. He wore the crooked buffalo calf's tail on his back, which showed that he would lure the kill over the cliff this year.

Ten paces behind Winter Weasel were his mother and his brothers and sisters, with their three dogs pulling heavily loaded travoises.

In rank with the medicine man and his son, four lance-lengths distant on the side of the throwing hand, walked Rising Bull, the great chief of all the people. He walked not as the leader, but as one of the tribe. Twice a year Gray Wolf led the tribe to the same place for the buffalo kill. Rising Bull's work was to teach justice and wisdom. Gray Wolf's work was to teach strength and skill. Each had been trained from childhood for his calling. Now Winter Weasel, too, must learn to be a leader—Winter Weasel and his best friend, Jumping Fox.

Jumping Fox was the son of Rising Bull. Today he did not walk with his father, but among his brothers. He wore no headdress. Not until the sage bloomed again after the snows would he become a warrior.

Chief Rising Bull wore a small headpiece of buffalo horns and a forelock, and from it the feathers of eagles streamed down his back until they almost touched the ground. In his hand he carried the sacred spear with its flint head gleaming.

On both sides of the two great chiefs and the boy were the lesser chiefs and

warriors of the tribe. Each man walked a pace behind the man next to him, making a great wedge like the V of northern geese in flight. Ten paces behind each man walked his squaws, his children, and his dogs pulling the travoises.

Gray Wolf was watching for a good omen. A small band of buffaloes grazed toward the path of the oncoming hunters. He had watched them for some time. Now he sang:

Oh Great Spirit of all buffaloes,
Lead these wild kinfolk to our coming footsteps.
Make their shaggy heads cross the trail before us.
Let them leave a mark across our pathway.
Let them stamp the ground with many hoofbeats.

Gray Wolf sang for his people. They knew only their customs and beliefs. By proper use of those customs and beliefs, the chief led them. His mind was busy while he sang aloud. He was watching the country for signs to give to his people. With their belief in the signs, he could give them confidence to do their work well during the piskun or buffalo kill.

Winter Weasel's mind was busy, too. He remembered how he had spent the long summer in practice. He had put on the buffalo robe and, alone, he had gone out onto the plain where the buffaloes grazed. There he had learned to lure them. He had listened to their grunting and bawling, and learned to make the same sounds. He had waited patiently until the first buffalo moved toward him. Then he had walked on slowly, getting it to follow him. When one came, others had come, too.

Many times he had practiced, until his confidence grew stout and his heart knew no fear. Thus Winter Weasel had learned his lesson, the secret of buffalo magic.

Now, walking beside his father on the piskun trail, he dreamed of the days

ahead. And as he dreamed, the blood rushed happily through his body, and he walked tall, with his head held high. His legs moved in long, even strides, and each foot was placed squarely in front of the other.

His chest was expanded and his stomach held flat. Winter Weasel had fasted for two days. None of the men in the ranks of the warriors had eaten. Only the women and the children and the dogs had eaten, for they had burdens to carry.

When Gray Wolf came to the place where the small band of buffaloes had crossed, he stopped. When all of the people were still and the dust had settled, he raised his hand, holding the buffalo-tail mace high over his head, and said:

"Hear, oh people of Rising Bull. Listen to the will of the Great Spirit. Buffaloes have crossed here. They are not yet out of sight. That is a good omen. We will let them go. We will let them live. This is only a small band that can start a new herd for other years. From the big herd these buffaloes came from we will get our piskun.

"Now to make magic we must erase the path of the buffaloes behind them. We must stamp out their footprints. So, all of you people of Rising Bull, hear the word of Gray Wolf, your medicine chief:

"Drag your feet as you cross the path of the buffalo, and let not one hoofmark remain."

The cloud of dust rose high as the people dragged their feet.

When they had passed the trail crossed by the buffaloes, Gray Wolf sang again:

Oh, Great Spirit, you have seen us
  cross the path

And erase the hoofmarks of the buf-
  falo band of omen.
We have rubbed the writing of their
  hoofs from the earth's face.
Now their life line has been broken.
They must start a new herd.
Of the many left behind them,
To the piskun we will lure them.

Gray Wolf knew better than any man in the tribe that the lives of the Indians depended on the buffalo. Only the buffaloes could be killed in numbers sufficient to provide food and shelter for the winter.

The elk were too swift, and the deer and moose too hard to kill with throwing spears and short bows. The bighorn sheep and the antelope were even more wary of man than the deer. The bears and big cats were too scarce, and they did not taste so good as buffalo meat.

The Indians loved the wild animals. They killed them only for their needs. They believed the buffaloes were put on earth for their use. They had seen more buffaloes die in a heavy winter blizzard than they would kill in the piskun. But still the herds were plentiful.

The tribe had had a good omen. The people were happy as they marched on.

CHAPTER TWO

THE PLACE OF THE PISKUN

THE SUN WAS NOW OVERHEAD, and it was hot for an autumn day. The rolling sea of brown grass reached as far as the eye could see. Only to the west and northwest could the high mountains be seen. In the cool valleys of those high mountains the tribe had spent the hot summer months. After the buffalo kill, the people would go down to the banks of the Great River and spend the winter in the shelter of the trees. Each tribe had its winter and summer homes. As they moved back and forth between them, the Indians would stop at one of the many high places where the mountains gave way to the prairie, and drive a herd of buffaloes over a cliff, to get meat for the next season.

Winter Weasel knew, as they came to the edge of the cliff, that the people had walked the very path the buffaloes would follow. His father, Gray Wolf, stopped, and all of the tribe stopped, too. Because of the V-formation in which the people

had traveled, each warrior was close to where he would stand in the piskun.

Small heaps of stones formed a triangle. Each warrior stood near one of these heaps of stones. Only Winter Weasel, Gray Wolf, and Rising Bull and the four other chiefs stood at the edge of the cliff where the buffaloes would fall.

Gray Wolf turned and said, "Oh, people of Rising Bull, we have come to the piskun. We have come to the place of the buffalo kill, and all is well. The eagle told me the winds wait to help us. The wolf told me the buffaloes are fat and healthy this year. They run fast."

Winter Weasel know how his father had learned this. He could tell by the way the eagle glided through the air that there was little wind high up. The wolf had been lean, showing that not many weak or sickly buffalo stragglers had let him come close enough to them to make an easy kill. Winter Weasel listened to his father again.

"Mighty warriors and honored chiefs, you stand now at the sacred heap of stones which will be your station in the piskun. Put your medicine mark upon it, so that it will be known to you when we return after making camp."

Each man took from his head the symbol of his name and put it on the heap of stones before him. Some of the symbols were feathers, some were claws, some were teeth, some were skins or stones or shells or carvings on wood or bone. All were different, so each man would know his own place in the piskun.

"Our great chief, Rising Bull, and Chief Yellow Cloud, Chief Dog Tooth, Chief Laughing Water, Chief Little Snow, and I,

Gray Wolf, your medicine chief, will stand below where the buffaloes fall, so that none can escape. The young men and boys will help us. The women and children will skin the animals when we have finished.

"Winter Weasel, my first-born, will lure the buffaloes here this year. He will leap to the sacred ledge. Look, now he will show you!"

For many years this plan had been followed. The Indians had learned that it was much easier to lead a herd of buffaloes than to drive them. However, the leader was in danger of losing his life at any moment. He must be disguised by wearing a buffalo robe to cover his body, for the animals would not follow a man. When he had coaxed them to follow him, the leader must be able to run faster than the stampeding herd so that he would not be trampled to death.

The cliff was thirty feet high—much too high for a man to jump from safely. Some way had to be found for the leader to escape from the onrushing buffaloes at the very edge of the cliff.

Ten feet to the left of the center of the warriors' stations and about eight feet below the top of the cliff was a small ledge made by the erosion which had formed the bluff. To reach this ledge, Winter Weasel had to run at full speed to the edge of the cliff, dive headfirst, then turn his body in a complete somersault to land with his feet on the shelf of rock. This required great skill and daring.

The ledge itself was too small to protect Winter Weasel from the buffaloes, but the Indians had dug a little cave into the cliff so that a man or boy could crouch against the back wall, safe from the falling animals and the crumbling earth and tumbling stones. Winter Weasel would press his body against the wall of the cave until the last buffalo had fallen past him.

After the buffalo kill of last spring, Winter Weasel had practiced for hours every day so that he could learn how to land on the ledge. He had worked slowly at first, twisting and turning his body to guide it through the air. Then he ran faster and faster, and leaped in a single movement from the edge of the cliff to the ledge below. The buffalo robe was heavy and hot on his back and head, but he had learned to gather it close to his body as he jumped so that he himself looked like a buffalo tumbling over the cliff.

Now he would make the leap with all the people watching him.

Winter Weasel walked to the edge of the cliff, stretching his legs far behind him at each step, as if he were dancing.

His heart pounded in excitement. He tried to keep all fear from his mind. He

would not let himself think of missing the mark and falling, like the buffaloes, down the steep cliff to certain death below. He knew that he must not falter for one second, for if he did the roaring herd would push him before them in the piskun.

He jumped safely to the little ledge.

Winter Weasel climbed back to the top of the cliff and when he stood up, all the people shouted.

Gray Wolf felt a warm glow in his heart at his son's skill, and he was pleased by the people's cheers. But he knew that he must not show his pleasure and let the people become lazy and puffed up in their pride. Instead he must find work for them, to keep their minds alert.

"Hear, oh people of Rising Bull, sons of the buffalo," he said. "Those of you on the side of my spear-throwing hand go this way, and those of you on the side of the hand of my heart go that way, to meet us at the foot of the cliff and make camp."

The sun had moved to another measur-

ing point in the sky by the time the people had gathered again at the foot of the cliff in the quiet little valley.

A black she-bear and her cub had been digging for grubs when the people came, and slowly Winter Weasel drove them away. The two bears left without anger for there was no fear between the animals and the Indians.

When everyone had come to the foot of the cliff, Gray Wolf took from his medicine bag four long hairs from the beard of a white buffalo. After making a chant, he

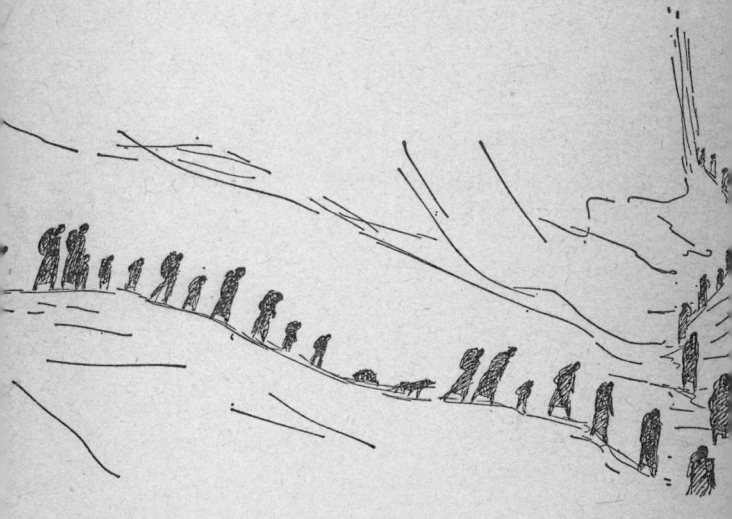

threw one hair to the north, one to the east, one to the south, and one to the west.

"Winter Weasel will tell you what the she-bear told him," said Gray Wolf.

Winter Weasel knew what his father meant. The bears were fat and their coats were long and sleek. They were ready for the winter ahead of them.

"The she-bear spoke to me," said Winter Weasel in a loud voice. "She told me how the moon god and the sun god had helped her find food all summer so that she would have much fat and a good warm coat for the long winter.

"She told me the moon god and the sun god would help us find food. Winter will come soon, she said, for the grubs are already deep in the cold ground."

The people nodded their heads. They knew the good omens of nature, and trusted the words of their wild brothers.

"Now we will make camp," said Gray Wolf.

Because the people came here twice a year, they knew what to do. Each family went to its old camp site and began to set up its tepee.

As soon as the chores were finished, the small children went to a little bank and

began to play their favorite game of buffalo-roll. They climbed to the top of the bank, tumbled over the edge and rolled down the hill, piling up at the bottom on top of one another. They laughed and shouted and played the game over and over again.

The chiefs and wise old men of the tribe went into the tepee of Gray Wolf. They sat still. No one said a word. When the light in the tepee grew dim, Gray Wolf spoke.

"We are all in accord," he said. "No one feels anger toward his brother. We will dance now, and tomorrow we will begin our council."

CHAPTER THREE

MOON MAGIC

Gray Wolf led the chiefs outside. They sat in a circle around a small campfire. Chief Laughing Water took a tom-tom. He began to beat on it slowly and steadily just as the moon rose in the east over the high cliff beyond the place of the piskun.

Laughing Water began the chant of welcome to the hunter's moon. When his song was over, the young men and boys, led by Winter Weasel, came out of their

tepees and made a large circle around another campfire. An old squaw threw some wood on the fire to make it blaze higher. The boys began to dance and sing. They sang the song of the coyote.

>   Oh Ye Wa, coyote brother,
>   Clever dog among the wild ones,
>   Little brother of the big wolf,
>   As the moon is to the sun.
>   Tell the moon, your foster father,
>   We will have his praise and blessing.
>   We will make ourselves his children.
>   We will make ourselves your brothers.
>   We will let you go unharmed

If he will make the buffaloes stay near
So we can lead them to our piskun.

Their voices were young and high, and sounded like the barking of coyotes, like a whole pack of coyotes yelping together.

The old men watched them as they danced. They joined in the singing and touched their hands to their mouths to accent the quaver of their voices. More tom-toms were played. The deep tones of the older men, singing and swaying their bodies back and forth around the small fire, and the high voices of the youths, circling the big fire in their dance, made a strange music in the wilderness.

Girls and old squaws peeked from tepee openings, and their eyes gleamed with excitement. Only the squaws who were to keep the fires high came out, to throw on more wood as it was needed. Then they went back into the tepees.

The dance lasted all night while the moon crossed the sky and set in the west. Gray Wolf rose to his feet in the light of the campfire and held both of his hands high over his head. The dancers stopped.

"The moon sleeps now," Gray Wolf said. "We will sleep, too."

He walked slowly to his own tepee and went in. All the other chiefs rose and went silently into their tepees. As the first rays of dawn showed in the eastern sky, all was still in the little valley. The dogs lay curled up outside the tepees where the people slept. The campfires were only red coals.

Winter Weasel was awakened by his father.

"My son," Gray Wolf said, "your sleep has been short, but we have much to do today, and the sun is already high in the sky."

Winter Weasel rubbed his eyes and threw back the buffalo robe under which he had slept so snugly. He had had a dream. He knew his father would take it as a good omen, so he told him.

"I dreamed a good dream," said Winter Weasel. "The eagle was so high in the sky that she went behind the moon. Then she flew down to me and told me that the

moon had a horn full of water behind her face."

"That means that when the moon is no longer full, it will rain," said Gray Wolf. "Let us write it upon the buffalo robe of history so that it will happen."

Gray Wolf spread the painted robe on the ground, and Winter Weasel took the colors and drew the symbols of his dream on it.

"Now we will show the people what they must do," said Gray Wolf.

The women and children had gathered

below, where the buffaloes would fall. Gray Wolf, Winter Weasel, Rising Bull, Yellow Cloud, Dog Tooth, Laughing Water, and Little Snow walked to the foot of the cliff. All the men of the tribe followed them.

"We stand where the buffaloes will fall," Gray Wolf told the people. "The first ones which come over the cliff will be killed at once. But as soon as enough buffaloes are piled up to make a landing place for the others, many will not be killed and will

try to run away. Chief Rising Bull will stand there, ready to spear any buffalo that comes his way."

Gray Wolf pointed to a large rock near the cliff. Rising Bull went to the rock and stood on it.

"Chief Yellow Cloud will stand there," said Gray Wolf. He pointed to another rock, and Yellow Cloud went to it.

Soon all five chiefs were standing on rocks that circled the place where the buffaloes would fall.

"If any buffalo escapes us, there will be

a strong defense line of young men and boys here," said Gray Wolf, and he walked in a half circle from one side of the cliff to the other. The young men and boys moved up to the places where Gray Wolf had told them to stand.

"No buffaloes must escape through this line," the medicine chief said. "The women and children will stay at a safe distance until the buffaloes are killed. Then they will come and help with the skinning.

"Now we will go to the top of the cliff to dance, and the women and children will return to camp. They will spend the time making drying racks for the meat and preparing for the feast after the piskun."

The chiefs and the warriors and Winter Weasel climbed to the top of the hill to the great magic circle where they would dance. The dance would last for two weeks, until the moon was gone.

CHAPTER FOUR

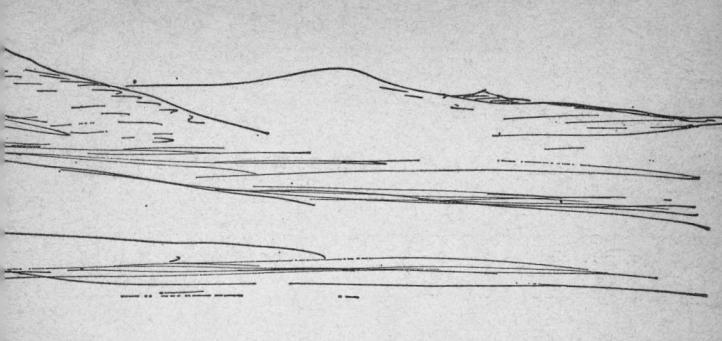

SWIFT AS LIGHTNING AND LOUD AS THUNDER

THE HIGH PLATEAU above the cliff where the chiefs and warriors and young men went for the great ceremonial dance was broad and had no trees or bushes of any kind. It was a sea of grass. Now in the October season, the grass had ripened to a golden brown.

The Indians went to the place of the dance in a long single file. Each man carried something that was magic, to sacrifice in the ceremony. Each chief wore his finest headdress and around his neck carried the pouch of sacred bones which told his name and his father's name and his grandfather's name. For every man was proud of his family. Each family had a chief who spoke for it in the council. The chief was always the oldest son of the oldest son. The other people were his brothers and sisters and wives, and their children.

Each baby boy born was to marry the next baby girl born into the tribe after him. Upon their marriage, the girl became a member of the boy's family. But only the men kept a record of their ancestors, through their fathers. The squaws kept no records.

There were nine chiefs in the council of the tribe; therefore, there were nine families. Everyone belonged to one of these families. Each chief was responsible for his family. Some of the families had many men in them, and some had only a few.

Now, as they walked through the grass,

the men of each family were together. First came the chief, the oldest son of the oldest son, and then came the next oldest son of the next oldest son. Each man knew his position and took pride in it.

Winter Weasel was the oldest son of Gray Wolf who had been the oldest son of his father, Western Wind. In their family, sixteen men were allowed to take part in the ceremonial dance. Two of the men were very old and wise. They were Gray

Wolf's uncles, for they had been Western Wind's brothers.

As they came to the place of the dance, the men took their usual positions. Gray Wolf raised his hands high in the air. All the men sat down and bowed their heads. They were silent while Gray Wolf spoke.

"Oh, mighty men of the buffalo tribe," the medicine chief began.

The tribe of Rising Bull called themselves the Buffalo People though Indians from faraway places called them the Blackfeet.

"The day is going and night is coming upon us," Gray Wolf went on. "We must now prepare for the dance. Pull up the grass where you are sitting and put the white powder of the moon upon the ground."

For a longer time than any man could remember, the tribe had made this great circle for their dance. In the spring, they danced among the charcoal ashes of their fires, and they made the great circle black

to represent the symbol of the sun and summer. In the autumn, they marked the great circle with white clay, the symbol for the moon and winter. In both seasons the buffaloes were lured over the same cliff.

The men pulled up the grass around them and threw it as far as they could. Each man had brought with him the bleached skull of a buffalo and a little bag

of white clay. He set the skull at the outer edge of the circle and spread the clay on the bare earth from which the grass had been pulled.

In the long, low glow of sunset, the white skulls gleamed in a great circle three hundred feet across. The white clay made a track that was easy to see in the brown grass. There was no fire so, as the moon rose in the dark sky, the white clay became the guide to the dancing feet.

The dance told the story of the people: how they had followed the buffaloes over the mountains into this valley, and how they needed the buffaloes for food, for clothes in the winter, and for robes and tents. All night the men danced. Each night the moon became smaller and smaller and its light less and less until, after two weeks, the moon was gone.

The weather had been very hot and for two days thunderclouds had been gathering in the sky. Gray Wolf told the people the clouds had promised him rain.

"It is a good omen," he said. "The light-

ning tells of the swiftness of the buffalo, and the thunder tells of the hoofbeats and greatness of the herd we shall lure."

The storm was short, but it was as wild as the dance of the Indians. The wind whipped the long grass and the thunder crashed against the hills. When the storm was over, Gray Wolf called all the people together.

"The rain has washed the land of old magic," he told them. "Now we will make new magic to give us success tomorrow. The sun is low in the western sky. Soon it

will be dark. This is the last night before the great buffalo kill.

"Winter Weasel will clear the way of the moon's path," Gray Wolf said. "He will seal the steps of all the dancing."

Winter Weasel lay down in the white clay of the great circle and began to roll along it. He rolled over and over and over, until he had rolled all the way around the circle and was once more at the place where he had started. The clay was wet and sticky, and Winter Weasel was covered with it from head to foot.

When he stood up, all the men went past him and touched him with their thumbs, to rub some of the clay from him. Then the men put their thumbs on their temples to signify the horns of a buffalo.

By the time all of the men had passed him, most of the clay was gone from Winter Weasel. He leaped into the air, and then began to dance. He twisted and turned and bent low and raised his feet high. He whirled and twirled and wove in and out among the people. Then he

jumped high into the air and fell in a heap upon the ground.

Two strong men brought a buffalo robe and wrapped him in it. Winter Weasel must rest so that he would be strong for the great run which would take place the next day. He slept.

CHAPTER FIVE

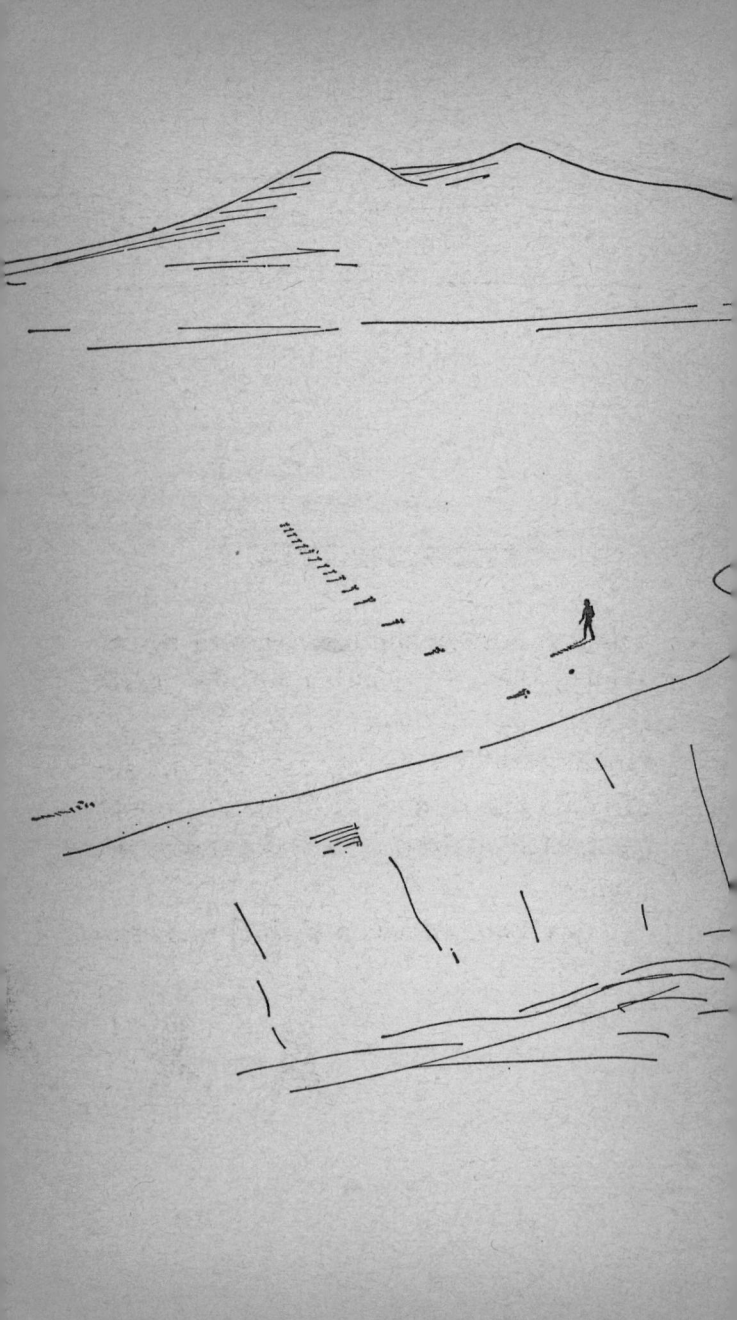

THE STAMPEDE

The sun rose in the clear eastern sky as Winter Weasel rolled out of the warm buffalo robe. He would not eat today before he led the buffaloes to the piskun. He picked up the buffalo skin which he would wear, and walked alone out onto the prairie.

Every man, woman, and child was care-

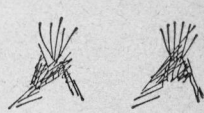

ful not to look at him, for to do so would have been bad luck. They busied themselves with work around their tepees and in the woods by the creek and along the base of the cliff. Soon Winter Weasel was on the plateau above the cliff. When enough time had passed for him to be out of sight, Gray Wolf gave the signal for the people to take their places. Everyone must be ready. No one must fail to do his duty. Yet the tribe knew that the most important person today was Winter Weasel.

Scouts had gone out each day to watch for the great buffalo herd. They had told Winter Weasel that the animals were a mile to the north of the camp.

As he walked toward the grazing place, Winter Weasel talked to the animals he saw on the way. A little herd of antelope was feeding on the flat prairie.

"My brothers, fleetest of all wild folk, give me some of your swiftness. Help me today to run as fast as you do," Winter Weasel said.

The antelope raised their heads and looked at him.

"I see," he said, "since you have not run from me when I asked you to share your swiftness with me this day, that you will gladly give some of it to me. For this I thank you, my brothers."

The antelope lowered their heads and returned to their grazing as Winter Weasel went on his way.

A badger, going to his den, looked at Winter Weasel as he passed.

"Brother Badger, most respected of the

weasels," he said, "give me this day some of your ability to hold on, so that I will not fail."

The badger let his eyes roll up and down so that he could see the full height of Winter Weasel.

Winter Weasel said, "Thank you, my brother. Your eyes tell me that you have looked at me and not found me wanting in strength. I go on with greater courage." And he walked on.

He came to a little rise on the plain, and a fox trotted across his path. It ran ahead of Winter Weasel and leaped upon a rock and sat down.

"You are known for your cunning, red brother," said Winter Weasel. "You have plenty of it and can, without harm to yourself, share it with me. Today I go to lure our kinfolk, the buffaloes, to the piskun so that my people can have their meat for food, and their brains and lungs to tan the hides for our clothes and tepees and sleeping robes. We must be well fed and

warm when the cold winds and snows come."

The fox sat still and watched Winter Weasel as he walked closer. When the boy was almost beside him, the fox jumped from the rock, turned a somersault, and disappeared. In a few seconds he came into view farther ahead and looked back at the young Indian.

"Thank you, brother fox," said Winter Weasel. "You have shown me your cunning and I see that you have plenty to

spare. I will use it well, for my people depend on me this day.

"For two long weeks we have danced to please the moon god who rules the wintertime when the nights are longer than the days. We have told him that our people need the buffaloes for food in his season. We did not use cunning on the moon, but I need cunning today to lure the buffaloes. Again, thank you, my brother."

The fox did not move, but watched the boy walk on his way.

When he came to the top of a second little rise, Winter Weasel saw the great

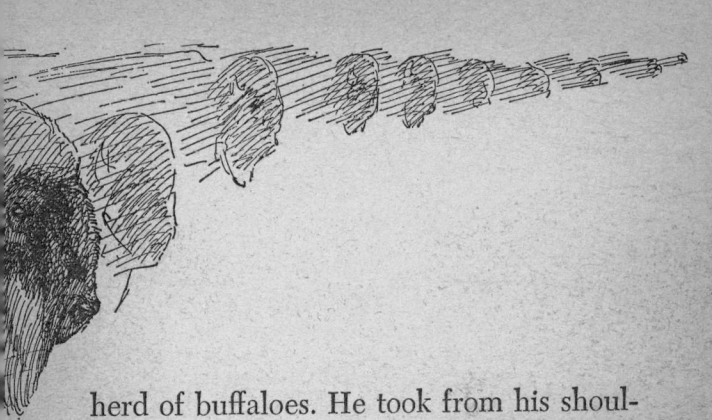

herd of buffaloes. He took from his shoulder the robe he was carrying, and opened it and threw it over his back. He placed the headpiece with the short horns on his head and tied the leg straps to his arms and ankles. He pulled the skin close around his body and hugged it to him.

Bending in a crouch, with his head lowered, he walked among the buffaloes as one of them. They paid no attention to him as he crept toward the leaders of the herd. The animals moved slowly northward as they grazed, and Winter Weasel knew he must turn them to the south, toward the piskun, before he started the stampede.

The long hours of practice had taught him to be patient. He walked back and forth between the two big bulls and brushed against their sides. They turned away from him, and he guided them slowly in a half circle until the whole herd was grazing southward.

Winter Weasel rested for a few minutes, stretching his muscles from the cramped position of the crouch. He breathed deeply to fill his lungs with the cold, clean air. He knew that when he began to run there would be no time to think of anything else.

The buffaloes grazed contentedly, and the boy looked at them with approval. There must be nearly a thousand in the herd. His people would have all the food and skins they needed.

Now he must begin the stampede. He walked behind the largest bull and brushed his side, as he had done before to turn him. This time, however, he walked in front of the animal, to attract his attention. The bull raised his head for a moment, then went back to his grazing. Winter Weasel grunted, and the beast looked up again. The boy jumped up and down and flapped the buffalo skin against his body.

The bull pawed the earth and took a few steps toward the strange moving object. Winter Weasel grunted again and walked backwards. The other leaders had stopped grazing and now watched him. They moved toward the big bull. The

whole herd seemed to feel that danger was near.

Winter Weasel felt a shiver of excitement run through his body. He had practiced this part many times, and he knew that now he had the attention of the leaders. But never before had he raced in front of them.

He turned his back to the great beasts and began to walk steadily toward the piskun. He did not need to look back to know that the buffaloes were following him. The sound of their hoofbeats told him that the stampede had begun.

Winter Weasel broke into a trot, and the buffaloes began to trot, too. They were about a mile from the piskun, and he knew that the next few minutes would be the most important ones in his life.

He swung into an easy loping run. He knew that the buffaloes would follow wherever he led them. Now he must use every ounce of his strength to stay in front of them and make the leap safely from the edge of the cliff to the ledge.

Already he could see the men at the little heaps of stones. As he ran past them, the men rose and waved wolfskins to keep the herd in line.

The buffaloes came closer and closer. They were gaining on Winter Weasel and the cliff still seemed far away. He must use all of his strength to keep ahead of the animals.

A ground squirrel's hole made the earth crumble as he stepped on it, and he lost his balance. The buffalo robe slipped from his shoulders. As he tried to pull it back, his leg twisted and he fell forward. Quickly, he doubled his body into a ball and rolled forward, as he had done many times when he was a small child playing games. He rolled over twice before he landed on his feet again.

A shout went up from the lines of warriors and lesser chiefs who formed the V-shaped guard on the cliff. Winter Weasel knew that the men were cheering for him.

But he had no time to think. The thundering tons of roaring flesh were bearing

down on him. The buffalo skin on his body was heavy and hot, and the straps around his ankles seemed to hold him back, pulling him toward the herd of running beasts.

The roar of the hoofbeats was louder to his ears than any thunder he had ever heard. The whole cliff shook, and the push of the air from the mass of shaggy heads nudged him on. Winter Weasel could feel the hot breath of the animals behind him. He ran on, heedless of the pain in his ankle.

CHAPTER SIX

THE PRAYER OF THANKS

Winter Weasel came to the edge of the cliff. He made the leap, as he had practiced it so many times, and landed on the ledge. Quickly he scrambled into the little cave at the back of the ledge.

The great brown bodies of the buffaloes pitched from the cliff and fell past the ledge. On and on they came, bawling and grunting, to land far below.

Winter Weasel breathed hard from the long run. The excitement of success made his heart beat faster. He sat on his injured ankle and put his other moccasined foot in the entrance of the cave. Leaning forward, he turned his head and watched the buffaloes tumbling through the air.

He shouted the call of the wolf who has made a kill. He cried the wail of the cougar crouched over his victim. He bellowed the roar of the grizzly bear who, with one blow of his mighty forearm, has downed a great buffalo bull. But his shouts

were lost in the thundering roar of the hoofbeats of the oncoming buffaloes. Their bawling as they fell from the cliff and the thuds of their bodies as they landed below filled the air with a deafening noise.

On top of the cliff, the warriors and lesser chiefs shouted, and the great chiefs and the men and boys below added to the noise.

Then there were no more hoofbeats on the plain above the ledge. No more buffaloes fell. The shouting had ceased. The only sounds were the groans of the dying buffaloes.

Winter Weasel crawled out of the cave and stood on the ledge of rock. Lifting his arms, he sang in a loud voice:

Oh, Great Spirit of the buffalo,
You have blessed me this day.
You have made the buffaloes follow me.
You have given us meat for the winter.
You have given us robes for warm beds.
You have given us hides for our tepees,
To keep out the snows.

You have kept us alive.
For all of this, we thank you.
We thank you with all our hearts.

For a moment there was stillness, then the people began to shout. The brave men who had stood behind the heaps of stones came to the edge of the cliff, and some of them reached down and pulled Winter Weasel from the ledge. Two strong men set him upon their shoulders and marched to the path that led to the foot of the cliff.

The rejoicing voices of the tribe filled the valley.

CHAPTER SEVEN

ENOUGH FOR ALL

WINTER WEASEL WAS CARRIED DOWN from the cliff. The chiefs and the boys who had stood in the great outer circle were pulling the buffaloes away to be skinned. It had been hard to prevent all of the animals from escaping. Many of them were still alive. The dogs had been tied up during the stampede, but now they were turned loose. There was great excitement.

Suddenly Jumping Fox shouted and pointed to a white buffalo calf. The calf had fallen on the bodies of the other buffaloes and had not been hurt. It scampered away now, but Jumping Fox and some of the other boys quickly caught it.

"It is a good omen," said Gray Wolf. "We will let the white calf go free in memory of the first buffalo kill of Winter Weasel. We will let the white calf become his symbol, for in manhood his name shall be White Calf."

The people shouted their agreement.

The rest of that week the people

worked, skinning the buffaloes. They used sharp stone knives and axes to cut the thick hides down the legs and along the bellies. Then they peeled the hides from the great bodies. The hides were stretched out to dry, if the fur was to remain on them for rugs and blankets. If buckskin was wanted for clothes and tepees, the hides were rolled into light balls, to start the hair-stripping. The brains and lungs of the animals were saved to be used in tanning the leather.

The meat was cut into thin strips to dry. The stomachs, hearts, kidneys, and livers were eaten at once in the great feast.

There was happiness in the camp. The children ran from place to place, doing what they were told to do. The women worked at cutting the meat. The men hung the strips of meat on the drying racks. Everyone was busy.

The wild animals were allowed to help themselves to the buffalo meat. There was enough food for all. Some bones were set

at the edge of the camp for the coyotes and wolves. Bears came at dusk and dawn, and dragged away whole carcasses. Eagles and hawks and magpies flew down and took what they wanted, and no one drove them away.

When all the buffaloes were skinned and the meat was cut from the bones and hung to dry, Gray Wolf called the people together.

Winter Weasel was to be declared a young man and have his name changed.

The chiefs sat in a half circle, and behind them sat the women and the children and the older men of no rank. Winter Weasel sat on the ground, facing all the people. He was dressed in the finest clothes of his boyhood. Beside him stood Gray Wolf.

"People of Rising Bull," said Gray Wolf, "you have seen my first-born son go out as a boy to the buffalo herd and lure it over the cliff."

A grunt of approval came from the people.

"Was it an act worthy of a man?" asked Gray Wolf.

The grunt of approval was louder.

Gray Wolf turned to Winter Weasel and said, "My son, I am happy to call you a man and to give you a man's name. In

your boyhood, you were known as Winter Weasel. It was a good name and you lived up to it.

"You have not been afraid to do things for your own good and for the good of our tribe. Your deeds up to now are written on the buffalo robe of history as those of Winter Weasel. Now you are a man, and you will be called White Calf. Go into the tepee and put on the clothes of a man."

The boy rose slowly. He looked at all the people before he walked into the tepee. Inside he found new clothes his mother had made for him. He took off the leggings and shirt of a boy and put on those of a man. There was a fringe on the shirt which was embroidered with porcupine quills and the ivory teeth of a bull elk.

When he was dressed, he went back to his father.

"My son, the clothes of a man become you," said Gray Wolf. "As a man—a young man now, a middle-aged man later, and an old man after many, many snows—you will be called White Calf."

Gray Wolf took a chain of bones and put it around White Calf's neck. From the chain hung a carving of a white buffalo calf made from a bleached buffalo skull.

Then Gray Wolf turned and went into his tepee to write on the buffalo robe of history.

All the people rose and walked past White Calf, and as they passed him, each one said, "Welcome, White Calf."

That night, after the tribe had eaten and danced, Gray Wolf stood up among the people sitting around the great campfire.

"People of Rising Bull, hear the words of your medicine chief," he said. "We have been favored in the buffalo kill. We have shared our bounty with our wild kinfolk. Now it is time for us to move on. My work is done. Tomorrow Rising Bull will lead us to our winter camp."

The next morning the long shadows reached out over the wild land, the desolate region where the prairie met the mountains. At the foot of a cliff lay a great heap of bones. A wolf dragged a buffalo's skull from the heap. An eagle soared in the air, holding a piece of meat.

To the south a cloud of dust moved away. The tribe was leaving, with Rising Bull, the chief, leading it. Now the people did not walk in formation. All of them carried packs and their dogs pulled travoises heavily laden with "green" skins and newly dried meat.

Among the people walked a young Indian. Two days ago he had been a boy. Now he was a young man. Then he had been called Winter Weasel. Now he was called White Calf.

White Calf wore the clothes of a man:

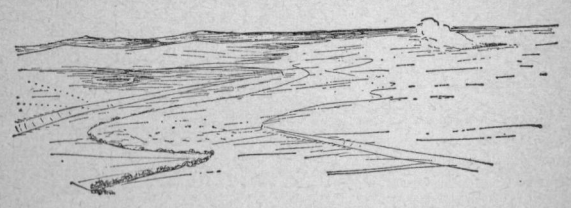

traveling moccasins, long leggings, and a shirt with fringe. From his hair hung three long white hairs from the tail of the white buffalo calf that had been set free as a good omen.

WASHINGTON SQUARE PRESS, INC.
ARCHWAY
PAPERBACKS

Other titles you will enjoy

29022 THE BLACK STONE KNIFE, by Alice Marriott. Illustrated by Harvey Weiss. Wolf Boy, a Kiowa Indian, takes an adventurous journey through a strange, new land. He meets his first white man, makes a daring escape from Apaches, and has a deadly battle with a water monster. (50¢)

29027 THE SECRET OF GRANDFATHER'S DIARY, by Milton Lomask. Illustrated by W.T. Mars. At his Grandmother's house, Denny solves a strange and baffling mystery involving an unknown thief who steals nothing but seemingly worthless old toys. (50¢)

29026 LITTLE VIC, by Doris Gates. Illustrated by Kate Seredy. A young man's courageous struggle to qualify as a jockey and to ride the horse he loves to victory. (50¢)

29021 KIM OF KOREA, by Faith Norris and Peter Lumn. Illustrated by Kurt Wiese. When Kim sets out on a long journey to find his American friend, he travels on the road to adventure where he makes friends with strolling acrobats and even helps capture a dangerous river pirate. (50¢)

29017 HAWAIIAN TREASURE, by Vanya Oakes. Illustrated by Isami Kashiwagi. A Boy Scout from the Mainland joins a troop in Hawaii, goes on a wild-pig hunt, a spear fishing trip, and ends up exploring for hidden treasure. (50¢)

29012 WILLY WONG: AMERICAN, by Vanya Oakes. Illustrated by Weda Yap. Knowledge of and pride in his Chinese heritage—as well as his love for baseball—helps Willy to make many new friends among his classmates. (50¢)

29006 THE LOST KINGDOM, by Chester Bryant. Illustrated by Margaret Ayer. Alone in the heart of the deep Green Jungle of India, a modern Hindu boy faces danger from tigers, raging boars, and elephants as he searches for the answer to an ancient mystery. (50¢)

29015 THE JIM THORPE STORY: *America's Greatest Athlete*, by Gene Schoor. Illustrated with photographs. The greatest all-around athlete of this century and his spectacular record in football, baseball, field and track. (50¢)

29007 MARCO POLO, by Manuel Komroff. Illustrated by Edgard Cirlin. The famous explorer who penetrated the exotic East and witnessed the splendor and squalor, culture and savagery of the fabulous world of Kublai Khan. (50¢)

(If your bookseller does not have the titles you want, you may order them by sending the retail price, plus 10¢ per book for postage and handling to: Mail Service Department, Washington Square Press, Inc., 1 West 39th Street, New York, N. Y. 10018. Please enclose check or money order—do not send cash.)